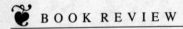

BOOK REVIEW

Here's what people are saying:

*Children will be amused by the incidents
. . . and will love the suspense and
adventure. . . .*

from SCHOOL LIBRARY JOURNAL

Weekly Reader Books presents

◆

JEFFREY'S GHOST

and the Fifth-Grade

DRAGON

◆

DAVID A. ADLER
Illustrated by
JEAN JENKINS

Henry Holt and Company ◆ New York

Published by arrangement with
Henry Holt and Company.
Weekly Reader is a trademark of Field Publications.
Printed in the United States of America.

Published by Henry Holt and Company,
521 Fifth Avenue, New York, N.Y. 10175

Library of Congress Cataloging in Publication Data

Adler, David A.
Jeffrey's ghost and the fifth-grade dragon.
Summary: Bradford the ghost goes to school with
Jeffrey and Laura when they begin fifth grade, and
being both mischievous and invisible he creates a lot
of problems.
1. Children's stories, American [1. Ghosts—Fiction.
2. Schools—Fiction] I. Jenkins, Jean, ill. II. Title
PZ7.A2615Je 1985 [Fic] 85-886

ISBN: 0-03-069281-4

Designer: Victoria Hartman

To Marc, Michele,
and Melissa

Jeffrey's Ghost and the Fifth-Grade Dragon

Chapter

◆ 1 ◆

"Hey, give me back my notebook," Jeffrey Clark called.

Jeffrey was walking to school with his friend Laura Lane. His notebook was floating in the air, just out of reach. Jeffrey felt something pull on his lunch bag. Then the bag flew out of his hands and floated next to the notebook.

The notebook and the lunch bag floated up and over an older boy's head. The boy looked up. The bag turned upside down. It opened, but nothing fell out. The boy jumped and tried to grab the lunch, but it moved out of reach.

"Whose lunch is this?" the boy asked.

"Mine," Jeffrey said softly.

"How do you do it? How do you make it fly like that?"

"It's the angel cake he has for dessert," Laura told the boy. "You know how angels are. They love to fly."

The older boy shook his head and walked away. Then Jeffrey whispered to Laura, "I'm glad you didn't tell him about Bradford."

Jeffrey's notebook and lunch weren't really floating. Bradford was carrying them. People could see Bradford until he was ten. Then, while he was cleaning a barn, a horse kicked him. That's when he became invisible. Bradford is a ghost.

After the horse kicked Bradford, he made his home in the hayloft of the barn. Then, many years later, the barn was torn down and a big yellow house was built. Bradford moved into a room on the second floor of the house. Many years later Jeffrey and his parents moved into that house. That's when Jeffrey met Bradford.

The notebook and lunch flew ahead of Jeffrey and Laura. Then the notebook and lunch dropped down. They floated close to the ground, past a small, gray kitten. The kitten smelled the lunch and ran after it.

The lunch flew up and the kitten climbed a tree to try to reach it. The lunch and notebook flew ahead into the school building, but the kitten was stuck in the tree. It began to cry.

"That Bradford," Jeffrey said as he reached for the kitten. "He should be more careful." Jeffrey put the kitten on the ground and walked with Laura into the school building.

It was the first day of the new school year. The halls were crowded with children, parents, and teachers. A man was standing in the middle of the hall holding up a lunch and notebook. He was the principal.

"All right," he called. "Whose are these?"

The principal opened the lunch bag and asked, "Who has a cream cheese sandwich, a carrot, and orange slices for lunch?"

Laura whispered to Jeffrey, "Don't tell him it's yours. You'll get into trouble. You can share my lunch."

The principal opened the notebook. "All right, who's Jeffrey Clark?" he asked.

"I am," Jeffrey said.

"I don't want to see any more of your magic tricks," the principal told Jeffrey as he gave him his lunch and notebook. "I have children who can't find their rooms and teachers who can't find chalk. I don't need floating cream cheese sandwiches."

"Yes, sir," Jeffrey said. He held on to his lunch and notebook tightly as he walked with Laura to their classroom.

The door to the room was open. A boy and a few girls were already sitting at desks. A few others were standing just inside the door and talking.

A tall thin woman stood in front of the room. She had long brown hair and wore large wire-framed eyeglasses.

"I don't want to sit too close to the front," Jeffrey told Laura as he walked into the room.

Jeffrey sat at a desk near the back of the room. Laura put her books on the desk next to his.

"She looks nice," Jeffrey told Laura.

Laura put a finger to her lips and whispered, "Sh."

"She looks like the teacher I had in the second grade," Jeffrey said. "She was real nice. At the end of each day she read us a story."

Tap, tap, tap.

The teacher was tapping her desk with a pencil.

"You in the back, with the brown hair," she said, looking at Jeffrey. "Please copy the work I left for you on the board. And the rest of you, please, come in and sit at a desk."

Jeffrey looked at the board. Then he began to copy:

> This is the fifth grade, Class 5-H. My name is Mrs. Fender. Homework for tomorrow: Bring in a notebook that is divided into four sections.

"Dragon Lady," someone behind Jeffrey said. "She's a Dragon Lady."

Mrs. Fender turned and looked at Jeffrey. Jeffrey turned. But there was no one behind him.

Chapter

· 2 ·

The class was very quiet. Mrs. Fender handed out some cards that Jeffrey and the others filled out. As Mrs. Fender collected them, she checked the names on the cards against the names in her roll book. Then Mrs. Fender picked up a sheet of paper and said, "Let me explain to you some of the rules of conduct in this class.

"Homework should be placed on my desk in the morning, as you enter the room."

Jeffrey felt something pull at his shirt. Then he heard Bradford whisper, "I once had a teacher like her. His name was Mr. Cotton. We called him 'The Dragon.' "

"Sh," Jeffrey said.

"You should come to school prepared for work. That means, you should come with pencils and your notebook. And, you should eat a good breakfast. You know, for children, break-

fast is the most important meal of the day. It gives you the energy to learn."

Bradford whispered, "The Dragon once found me eating during class. He made me stand in front of the class and say one hundred times, 'I will not chew cheese whenever I please. I will not chew cheese whenever I please.'"

"Quiet!" Jeffrey said.

"Young man," Mrs. Fender said as she looked straight at Jeffrey. "I am trying to talk to the class. I will be quiet as soon as I'm finished."

"I'm sorry, I wasn't talking to you," Jeffrey said softly.

"I will not chew cheese whenever I please," Bradford said a third time.

Mrs. Fender looked past Jeffrey. She looked around the room. Then she said, "Young man, you're making this first day of school very difficult for me. I don't think this is the place for you to practice making your voice sound like it's coming from someplace else. This is a school. You are here to learn."

"I will not chew cheese whenever I please," Bradford whispered. "I only have to say it ninety-six more times."

Mrs. Fender then turned to the class, smiled, and said, "Since today is the first day of school, I decided not to begin with a regular lesson. When I call on you, I'd like each of you to stand, tell us your name and something funny or interesting that happened to you during the summer. I'll begin."

"I will not chew cheese whenever I please," Bradford whispered again.

Mrs. Fender looked down for a moment, as if she was thinking. Then she said, "This summer I learned to use a computer. Now I use it to write all my lessons."

Mrs. Fender smiled at a girl in the front row. She stood.

"The Dragon told scary stories," Bradford whispered. "When we screamed, he laughed."

"Sh," Jeffrey said, and Mrs. Fender looked at him.

"My name is Janet Maple," the girl standing said. "And this summer I went to day camp. The only really great thing that happened there was one day the camp director was showing some parents the camp. He took a few steps back to show them the view, and he fell into the pool."

"We once threw The Dragon into the pond," Bradford told Jeffrey.

Mrs. Fender heard Bradford talking. She walked toward Jeffrey. When she was halfway down the aisle she asked, "What's your name?"

"Bradford."

"Jeffrey Clark."

"Well, Bradford Jeffrey Clark, you don't seem to be able to sit quietly."

"I'm sorry," Jeffrey said.

Mrs. Fender was walking toward the front of the room when Bradford said, "Dragon Lady. You're the Fifth-Grade Dragon."

"That's it," Mrs. Fender said. "You'll have to see the principal."

Mrs. Fender walked to her desk. She wrote a note and then went to the door. When the hall monitor walked past, she gave her the note. She asked her to take Jeffrey to the principal.

"I told you she was a Dragon Lady," Bradford said once they were in the hall.

"You keep getting me into trouble," Jeffrey said. "As soon as the principal sees me he'll say, 'Oh, so it's the boy with the floating cream cheese sandwich.' I may get thrown out of school!"

Chapter

· 3 ·

J effrey waited outside the principal's office. The door to the office was open. A woman and a small child were with the principal.

"I'm sorry," the principal said. "Betsy is too young to begin school."

"But she reads," the woman said.

"We don't take children for the first grade until they're at least five years old."

"Betsy writes."

"I'm sorry."

"Betsy can tell time, tie her own shoelaces, and play the violin."

The principal jumped out of his seat and said, "Look what she did. She wrote on the wall!"

"But look at the big word Betsy wrote. She wrote *cranberry*."

"Take her out," the principal said.

"And she spelled it right."

The principal pointed to the door and said, "Take her out now!"

As the woman picked up her daughter she said, "Tell the nice man what a cranberry is."

Betsy stuck out her tongue.

The woman carried her daughter out of the office. As the woman walked past Jeffrey, she told Betsy, "Just for that, you can't use the computer today."

"Next!" the principal called.

A teacher walked in.

"Something is wrong with the sink in my room. The water coming out of the faucet is green."

"Your art room was used during the summer. There's probably some paint stuck in the faucet. I'll have it fixed."

The teacher walked out.

"Next!" the principal called again.

The hall monitor led Jeffrey into the office. The principal was reading some papers. Then he looked up, saw Jeffrey, and said, "Oh, it's the boy with the floating cream cheese sandwich. What have you done now?"

The monitor gave the principal Mrs. Fender's note. Then he left the office.

The principal read the note, rubbed his eyes,

and said, "This is the first day of school. Couldn't you wait a few days before you got into trouble?"

Jeffrey didn't answer. He didn't know what to say.

"This note says you disturbed the class. It says that you threw your voice and called Mrs. Fender a dragon."

"I didn't really do that. Someone else said that. Mrs. Fender just couldn't see the person who was talking to me."

"No one can see me. I'm invisible," Bradford said. His voice came from the window ledge.

The principal turned. But of course he couldn't see Bradford.

There was a small cabinet next to the principal's desk. The principal opened it and took out a folder.

"Is your name 'Bradford Jeffrey Clark' or just 'Jeffrey Clark'?"

"Jeffrey Clark."

"Hmm."

Jeffrey stood quietly and waited while the principal read his school records. Then the principal looked up and said, "You did very well in your old school. There's no record here of any trouble at all, no floating sandwiches or invisible friends.

"I'm going to ask Mrs. Fender to take you back. But if you get into trouble again, your parents will have to come in and talk to me."

As the principal wrote a note to Mrs. Fender he said, "The proper place for your magic is on a stage. If we have a talent show later in the year, I expect you to be in it."

The principal gave Jeffrey the note. As Jeffrey left the office Bradford whispered, "Did you hear that! He wants you to be in a talent show."

"Now you listen to me, Bradford," Jeffrey said once they were in the hall. "If you get me into trouble again, I'll stop talking to you. I won't be your friend. I'll have nothing to do with you."

While Jeffrey was talking, two hall monitors walked past. "That kid is weird," one of them said. "He talks to himself."

"He's not just talking to himself," the other hall monitor said. "He's fighting with himself."

"Is it my fault that your teacher is a dragon?" Bradford whispered.

Jeffrey turned to the water fountain. That's where he thought Bradford was standing. Jeffrey pointed at the water fountain and said, "And I don't want to hear any more about chewing cheese whenever you please."

Jeffrey walked to the classroom. He stood by the door and waited for Mrs. Fender to notice him.

"My name is Laura Lane," he heard his friend tell the class. "I played on a baseball team this summer called the Ghosts, and we won the championship."

Laura sat down. Then Mrs. Fender turned and saw Jeffrey standing at the door.

Chapter

· 4 ·

Mrs. Fender walked to the door. She read the principal's note. Then she smiled and said, "He wrote that you have a good school record. If you think you can sit quietly, you may return to your seat."

Jeffrey walked quickly to his seat. He felt something tap him on his back. But Jeffrey didn't turn.

Mrs. Fender walked to the board. She wrote SALE in large letters. Then she drew a ruler, pencil, pen, notebook, and an eraser on the board. Under each she wrote a price.

"I have to talk to you," Bradford whispered.

Jeffrey looked straight ahead.

"Now, class," Mrs. Fender said. "For today's math lesson, let's do some shopping. How much would I have to pay for a notebook, ruler, and pen?"

Jeffrey opened his notebook. He picked up his

pencil, and it flew out of his hands. It floated up. Then it moved over the paper and wrote, *"I'm sorry. I'll try not to get you into any more trouble. Bradford."*

Jeffrey grabbed his pencil. He turned the page in his notebook and began to write.

"Two dollars and twelve cents," Barry answered.

"Now find the cost of four notebooks."

Jeffrey wrote the price of one notebook. He multiplied that number by four. When he had an answer, he raised his hand.

"Yes," Mrs. Fender said as she pointed to Jeffrey.

Jeffrey looked down at his paper. His answer had been erased. Jeffrey couldn't remember what he had written. *If one notebook costs a dollar fifty-seven*, Jeffrey said to himself, *then four notebooks cost . . .*

"Do you have an answer?"

Jeffrey was about to say, "No," when his pencil began moving. It wrote *"$6.28."*

"Six dollars and twenty-eight cents," Jeffrey said.

"Very good. Now find the cost of nine pens."

"You should thank me," Bradford whispered. "You had the wrong answer."

"Thank you," Jeffrey said.

Jeffrey sat next to Laura at lunch. While Jeffrey was holding his sandwich, he noticed it getting smaller. Bradford was eating it. Jeffrey took four big quick bites and pushed the rest of the sandwich into his mouth.

"Ing gnu gnatta ga gung bing goor gone," Jeffrey said with his mouth still full.

"What?"

Jeffrey swallowed. "I was just telling Bradford that if he wants a lunch, he should bring one."

In the afternoon Mrs. Fender told the class, "During the next few weeks we will be studying local history. Some of you may be surprised at the many interesting things that have happened here." Mrs. Fender sat on the edge of her desk and said, "I'd like each of you to write a report about our local history. You might want to write the history of our firehouse or about the old shoe factory on Grove Street."

"Could I write about the day my grandfather sat in a tree for one hundred hours?" Janet asked. "It was in all the newspapers."

"Yes."

"Could I write about my father's candy store?" asked another student. "It's more than fifty years old."

"Yes. And describe what the store was like fifty years ago."

"Can two people work together on a report?" Laura asked.

"Yes."

As Jeffrey and Laura walked home from school, they talked about the school report. Laura said, "Let's work together."

"But what will we write about?"

"Why don't you write about the town's first school," Bradford said. "It opened almost two hundred years ago."

"But where will we find out about an old school like that?" Laura asked.

"From me," Bradford said. "I was there when it opened."

Chapter

· 5 ·

"The schoolhouse was just one big room," Bradford told Jeffrey and Laura as they walked toward home. "The teacher's name was Mr. Cotton. We called him schoolmaster, and he stood behind a high desk in front. We didn't have desks. We sat on benches along the sides of the room. There was a fireplace with a chimney. But I sat along the back wall. The heat from the fire didn't reach me. I was real cold in the winter."

"How horrible," Laura said. "How did you study in the cold?"

"There were usually a few broken windows. The cold wind really blew in on us. But we studied. We had to. The first time Mr. Cotton saw one of us not doing his work, he yelled. The second time Mr. Cotton hit him with a stick. That's why we called him 'The Dragon.' "

"But Mrs. Fender is not like that," Jeffrey said.

"Maybe not. But she wears wire eyeglasses just like he did. And anyway, since the time I was in school, I call all schoolmasters dragons."

There was a bench at the corner. Jeffrey and Laura sat down.

"Did you get into a lot of trouble in school?" Jeffrey asked Bradford.

"Yes. But my friend James was worse than I was. He was always getting into trouble.

"We had a bucket with drinking water near Mr. Cotton's desk. One morning, before he came in, James put a live frog in the bucket. 'He'll never know who did it,' James told me."

"What happened?" Laura asked.

"Just as the schoolmaster walked into the room, the frog jumped out of the bucket. Lots of kids screamed. But James and I didn't. We were laughing so hard, we couldn't stop. Mr. Cotton took his stick and banged it on his desk for quiet. Then he saw us laughing. We were both punished. We chopped firewood all week."

"But that wasn't fair," Laura said. "James put the frog in the bucket. You didn't."

Honk! Honk!

A bus had stopped. The door to the bus opened. The driver called, "Are you children getting on or not?"

"No. We're just sitting here," Jeffrey told the driver.

"This is a bus-stop bench," Jeffrey said after the bus drove off. "Let's sit someplace else. I don't want another bus to stop for us."

Jeffrey, Laura, and Bradford walked toward Jeffrey's house. As they walked, Bradford talked about his friend James.

"Once James put some flowers on Mr. Cotton's desk."

"That was nice," Laura said.

"No. It wasn't. Mixed in with the flowers was poison ivy. James hoped the schoolmaster would touch it and begin scratching."

"Did he?"

"No, but James did. It was real funny watching James that day. He didn't want Mr. Cotton to know that he put the poison ivy on his desk, so he couldn't scratch. But he itched real bad and he looked strange. His mouth was shut real tight and his eyes kept blinking. Mr. Cotton yelled at James to stop making funny faces."

Jeffrey and Laura sat on the front steps of Jeffrey's house.

"If you tell us everything that happened in school, we can write a great report," Jeffrey said.

Jeffrey took a pen from his pocket. He opened his notebook and put it on the step next to him.

"Once James really got me into trouble," Bradford said.

"Don't just tell us about James. We can't write a report about him. Tell us what you learned and things like that."

"I came into class and my bench was gone. James had buried it."

"I can't write a report on what James did with your bench," Jeffrey said.

"He buried it on Mr. Winter's farm, just inside the fence. I had to stand for more than two weeks."

"Why couldn't you dig up the bench?" Laura asked.

"Mr. Winter's bull was tied to that fence. I couldn't get near it."

Jeffrey's notebook closed. It floated up into Jeffrey's lap. Then Bradford sat on the step next to Jeffrey.

"Lots of interesting things were carved into that wooden bench top. I'd love to see it again," Bradford said. "Mr. Winter and his bull are gone. I'll bet we can dig up that old piece of wood."

Chapter
· 6 ·

The next morning as Jeffrey left his house he whispered, "Now don't get me into trouble today." But Bradford didn't answer.

Jeffrey was careful to hold on to his lunch as he walked. He didn't want it to float away again. But Jeffrey didn't feel anything pull at his lunch.

Jeffrey walked into the school building. The halls were crowded. Children were rushing to their classrooms. The principal was talking to a teacher. Jeffrey went to his classroom and sat at his desk.

"Is he here?" Laura whispered.

"I don't know," Jeffrey answered. "Bradford hasn't spoken to me and nothing strange has happened this morning."

Jeffrey began to copy the homework from the board. Then he whispered to Laura, "I'm worried. I don't know where Bradford is. He could be getting into some real trouble."

31

"Jeffrey Clark, please work quietly," Mrs. Fender said.

"I hope all of you brought a notebook with sections," Mrs. Fender said a few minutes later. "Please make the first part of your notebooks the 'Science' section."

Jeffrey wrote SCIENCE in large letters across the top of the first section of his book.

"Our first science lesson is on the weather," Mrs. Fender said. She told the class that the sun warms the earth. Summer is warmer than winter because there are more hours of sunlight during the summer. And during the summer the sun is directly over us.

Jeffrey and Laura sat together during lunch. Jeffrey unwrapped his sandwich and quickly took a few big bites. Laura looked at Jeffrey and laughed. His cheeks were puffed out. They were filled with his cream cheese sandwich.

"You don't have to eat so fast," Laura said. "No one else is going to eat your sandwich. Bradford isn't here."

After lunch Mrs. Fender taught the class math and grammar. Then, after the bell rang at the end of the school day, Laura went to Mrs. Fender's desk. Laura asked if she and Jeffrey

could write their local history report on the town's first school. "We'll also write what school was like in those days," Laura said.

"That's a wonderful idea," Mrs. Fender said.

On their way home from school a leaf fell from a tree and into Jeffrey's pocket. Jeffrey pulled it out and threw it onto the ground. A few more leaves and some twigs flew into Jeffrey's pockets. Jeffrey pulled them out and said, "Stop it, Bradford!"

"Don't you want to know where I was today?" Bradford asked.

"Yes," Laura said. "Where were you?"

"I went to the Winters' farm. A lot of houses were built on that farm. But I think I know just where that bench top is buried."

"You never told us how James was able to dig there," Jeffrey said. "Wasn't he afraid of the bull?"

"James did errands for Mr. Winter. He helped him with his planting and chopped wood for him. James must have been on the farm once when the bull was tied somewhere else. But every time I went there, the bull lowered his head and made noises like he was ready to charge at me. When he did that, I ran."

Jeffrey and Laura were about to cross the street when Bradford pulled them back.

"Turn here. Go down this street," Bradford said. "I'll show you where we have to dig."

They walked past a few stores and the firehouse.

"I remembered there was a big rock at the edge of Mr. Winter's farm. When I found that rock, I just counted the steps to where the corner fence was."

Bradford led Jeffrey and Laura to an old
house. The house had a large front lawn sur-
rounded by a wire fence. The house needed
paint. A few windows were broken and covered
with wood.

"I'm not digging in someone else's yard,"
Jeffrey said. "We don't need some old piece of
wood for our report. All you have to do is tell us
about your school."

"Well, I'm not telling you if you don't help me
dig up my bench," Bradford said.

Jeffrey leaned back against the fence.

"That bench would be great for our report,"
Laura said. "And we can be careful not to ruin
the lawn."

Grrr.

Jeffrey turned. A large brown dog was running toward him.

Chapter

· 7 ·

Jeffrey and Laura ran past two houses to a large oak tree. They hid behind the tree.

Arf! Arf!

Jeffrey and Laura waited. The dog barked again, but the barks didn't sound any closer. Jeffrey and Laura quietly turned and looked back at the dog. He was barking and jumping, trying to get over the fence. But he couldn't.

Bradford laughed and said, "That dog is a puppy. Mr. Winter's bull was ten times his size."

The dog barked again. Then he turned and walked back toward the house.

"I'll dig for that bench top myself," Bradford said. "I don't need your help."

"It's not right. It's not your yard," Jeffrey said. But Bradford was already gone.

Jeffrey and Laura sat by the oak tree and watched as a large shovel floated out of the garage of the old house. The dog followed the

shovel. The shovel started to dig a few feet from the fence. First it cut out a square from the grass. Then it dug a neat, deep hole. The dog sat and watched.

Bradford stopped digging. He put the dirt back into the hole. Then he placed the square of grass neatly over the dirt.

"He didn't find the bench," Jeffrey said.

The shovel moved a few feet over. It cut out another square of grass. Then it dug another deep hole.

"He might dig up that whole yard and not

find it," Jeffrey said. "Someone else may have found it fifty or a hundred years ago. Or maybe Bradford isn't even digging in the right yard."

Jeffrey and Laura walked closer. They stood near the fence and watched as Bradford dug two more holes. The second hole was very close to where the dog was resting. Then, as Bradford was filling it in, some dirt fell on the dog's tail.

The dog barked. He jumped up, ran in a circle and growled at the shovel.

"Good dog. Good dog," Jeffrey and Laura heard Bradford say. It didn't calm the dog. He kept running in a circle and growling.

"Hey, what's happening out there," they heard an old man call. He was walking toward them. The old man held out his hand and the dog ran to him. Then, with the dog at his side, the man walked to the fence.

"What are you children doing here?" the old man asked. "You've scared Pepper."

Then the old man saw the dirt on the ground and the shovel. "You ruined my lawn," he said. "And you used my shovel to do it!"

"We didn't do that," Jeffrey said. "We haven't been digging."

"What's that? I can't hear you."

"I said, 'We haven't been digging.' "

"Who's singing?"

Jeffrey shook his head and said real loud, "We haven't been digging!"

"You've ruined my lawn," the old man said. "I watered it all summer and weeded it, and now you ruined it."

The shovel floated up. It began to put the dirt back into the hole.

"Witchcraft! Witchcraft!" the man yelled.

The shovel put the square patch of grass over the hole.

"I'm calling the police," the old man said. Then he turned and ran toward his house.

Chapter

· 8 ·

"Quick. We have to stop him," Laura said. Jeffrey and Laura started to climb the fence. Pepper growled. Jeffrey and Laura stopped climbing. Jeffrey took a few steps back. Pepper growled again as Jeffrey opened his notebook and wrote:

> We did not dig in your garden. But
> we would be happy to help you replant
> the grass. We can do garden work and
> other errands.

"Bradford," Jeffrey called. "Bradford. You got us into this trouble. Now you better help us get out of it."

Jeffrey and Laura waited. But Bradford didn't answer.

"Bradford," Jeffrey called again. "You come here and help us."

"Look," Laura said as she pointed to a long piece of rope floating out of the garage. Laura and Jeffrey watched as one end of the rope seemed to tie itself into a knot around Pepper's neck.

"Come on," Bradford said. "I'll hold the dog. You run and give the old man your note."

The rope pulled at Pepper. Pepper pulled back.

"Let's hurry," Jeffrey said, "and catch him before he calls the police."

Jeffrey and Laura climbed over the fence. Pepper growled as they ran past. The dog pulled at the rope, but he didn't get away.

The old man was standing on the porch. He was searching through his key ring. "It's one of these keys," the man mumbled. "I know one of these will open the door."

Jeffrey handed him the note.

"What's this?"

"Read it," Laura said.

"Feed it?" the old man said and shook his head. "Feed it," he mumbled. "I wonder what she means." Then he read the note.

There was a rocking chair on the porch. The man sat in the chair. He looked up at Jeffrey and Laura. "What about the shovel?" he asked.

Laura laughed. "That's not witchcraft. That's magic. Jeffrey does lots of magic. He makes cream cheese sandwiches fly and things like that. He's going to be in the school talent show."

"I'm Jeffrey Clark," Jeffrey said.

"And I'm Laura Lane."

The old man smiled. "I'm Robert Denton," he

said. "And I'd like your help. We'll water the grass you dug up. Then you can help me plant some tulip bulbs. Fall is the time to plant bulbs, you know."

Jeffrey and Laura watered the grass. Then Mr. Denton showed Jeffrey and Laura how to plant tulips. They dug small holes along the fence. Then they gently put a tulip bulb into each hole and covered it with dirt.

"I've hit something," Jeffrey told Laura as he was digging.

"Maybe it's a rock."

"No," Jeffrey said as he reached down. "It feels like wood!"

Jeffrey started to dig more dirt out with his hands. But he still wasn't able to pull out the piece of wood. He picked up the shovel and dug some more.

"No, no, no," Mr. Denton said. "Tulips are small. You don't have to dig so much."

Jeffrey reached down and pulled out a flat, dark piece of wood. Jeffrey brushed off the dirt. Initials were carved all over one side of the wood.

"That's it," Bradford said. "That's my bench top."

"Look here," Laura said. "Here's your name. Bradford loves Darlene."

"That's not my name."

"Sure it is," Laura said. "Tell us about Darlene. Was she your sweetheart?"

"No."

"Was she pretty?"

"No."

"But you liked her."

"That's just another of James's jokes," Bradford told Jeffrey and Laura. "Darlene was Mr. Winter's mule."

Chapter

· 9 ·

Jeffrey and Laura cleaned the bench top. They wrote their report on the town's first school and gave it to Mrs. Fender. A few days later they read their report to the class.

"It wasn't easy going to school in those days," Jeffrey said as he read the report. "The whole school was in one room with one teacher. The teacher was called schoolmaster and he was usually a man. He took turns living with people who had children in his school. This town's first schoolmaster was Mr. Cotton."

Jeffrey described the classroom. Then Laura told the class what was taught in Mr. Cotton's school.

"The older children read from the Bible. The younger children listened. A lot of time was spent on spelling and writing practice. The children each had a notebook. They called it a

copybook. The schoolmaster would write on the top of a page in the copybook. He would write a motto like, 'Look before you leap.' The children would copy it again and again."

When Laura finished reading, Jeffrey held up the bench top and said, "This was in that first schoolhouse. A boy named Bradford sat on it while he did his schoolwork."

"Wonderful," Mrs. Fender said as she walked to the front of the room. "That report was very well done."

A few days later Jeffrey was in the principal's office again. Laura, Mrs. Fender, and Mr. Denton were with him. They were giving the bench top to the school. A newspaper reporter and a photographer were there too.

"This bench will be put in a glass case in the hall," the principal said. "And we'll put a copy of your report on our first school in the case too."

The photographer took a picture of the principal, Mrs. Fender, Mr. Denton, and Jeffrey and Laura holding the bench top.

Then the principal gave Jeffrey and Laura two cards. There was a gold star on each card. "I am also giving each of you these awards for your good work," he said.

The reporter and photographer were about to leave the office when the principal said, "Don't go yet. Jeffrey is a great magician. Maybe he'll show us some of his magic."

Just then the reporter's pen and notebook

flew out if his pocket and onto the principal's desk. Then a chair and Mr. Denton's hat floated onto the desk.

"How did you do that?" the reporter asked.

"Give me back my hat," Mr. Denton said.

"He didn't do it. I did," Bradford told everyone.

Bradford was standing behind the reporter. The reporter, the photographer, and Mrs. Fender turned. But they didn't see anyone.

"Give me back my hat," Mr. Denton said again.

"Aren't these kids great," the principal said as he took the chair off his desk.

"I'm great too," Bradford said as the principal's desk drawer opened. A blank award card floated out.

No one saw Bradford. It seemed that the reporter's pen was writing without anyone's help. It wrote Bradford's name on the card.

"I want my hat!" Mr. Denton said.

The reporter scratched his head and said, "I would write in my newspaper article about the floating chairs and pens, but no one would believe it. No one would believe it."

Just then the hat floated off the principal's desk and landed on Mr. Denton's head. He held on to it with both hands and said, "Thank you."

Union Times Gazette   Page 3B

BrAdford + DArlene

Fifth-grade students, Jeffrey Clark and Laura Lane, holding school bench seat. In rear, Mrs. Fender, Mr. Denton, and school principal.

School News ..

ABOUT THE AUTHOR

David A. Adler is an editor for a New York publishing house and the author of more than thirty books for children, including the popular Cam Jansen series. He lives in Woodmere, New York, with his wife and son.

ABOUT THE ILLUSTRATOR

Jean Jenkins is a children's book illustrator who also runs a graphic arts studio with her husband in Cochecton Center, New York.